Tivnan

GRANDMOTHER'S GARDEN

BY JOHN ARCHAMBAULT
ILLUSTRATED BY RAÚL COLÓN

Silver Press
Parsippany, New Jersey

To Grandma Rose and her rose garden,
who lived on Sunnyslope Drive in Pasadena, California
and gave me her daughter,
my mother, Shirley Jean Hart.
J.A.

Text copyright © 1997 by John Archambault
Illustrations ©1997 by Raúl Colón
Cover and book design by Michelle Farinella

Published by Silver Press
A Division of Simon & Schuster
299 Jefferson Road,
Parsippany, New Jersey 07054-0480

Printed in the United States of America.

Library of Congress Cataloging-in-Publication Data
Archambault, John
Grandmother's garden/by John Archambault: illustrated by Raúl Colón.
   p. cm.
   Summary: Grandmother Rose's garden provides a place for children of
different backgrounds to meet and become friends.
      [1. Gardens—Fiction. 2. Individuality—Fiction. 3. Stories in rhyme.]
I. Colón, Raúl, ill. II. Title.
PZ8.3.A584Gr 1997   96-3469
[E]—dc20   CIP   AC
ISBN 0-382-39652-9 (LSB) 10 9 8 7 6 5 4 3 2 1
ISBN 0-382-39653-7 (JHC) 10 9 8 7 6 5 4 3 2 1

Roses, carnations, chrysanthemums—
In Grandmother's garden, we are all one.

She tenders us, gentles us, nurtures us with care.

Born from the earth with water and air,
Born from the earth with water and air.

Earth is a garden turning 'round the sun,
With room to bloom for everyone.

We're all flowering faces reaching for the sun.

In Grandmother's garden, we are all one.
In Grandmother's garden, we are all one.

We are one, we are one.
In Grandmother's garden, we are one.
Turning 'round the sun,
We are one.

Grandma Rose used to say to me,
"Feel the earth on your hands and knees.

Till your fingers through the soil 'til the time stands still,"
In Grandmother's garden.

It all starts from a tiny seed.
A little patch of earth is all we need.

Fresh river water or falling rain,
A little bit of sunshine and lots of love.
A little bit of sunshine and lots of love.

Different colors, different faces, different names—
Underneath our skin, we are all the same.

We are flowering faces reaching for the sun.
In Grandmother's garden, we are all one.
In Grandmother's garden, we are all one.

We are one, we are one.
In Grandmother's garden, we are one.
Turning 'round the sun,
We are one.

Grandma Rose used to say to me,
"Feel the earth on your hands and knees.

Till your fingers through the soil 'til the time stands still,"
In Grandmother's garden.

Joseph, Camille, and Alexandria—
In Grandmother's garden, we are all one.
She tenders us, gentles us, nurtures us with care.

Born from the earth with water and air,
Born from the earth with water and air.

José from Mexico, Celine from France,

David, Mohammed, Sarah, and Hans,

Stanley, Tyler, Michael, and Collette,

Sergei, Kevin, Keiko from Japan,

In Grandmother's garden, we are all one.

We are one, we are one.
In Grandmother's garden, we are one.
Turning 'round the sun,
We are one.